For Jaden and Weston Ow to read to their grandparents,
George and Gail

With special thanks to Mary Lee Donovan, Heather McGee,
Laura Rivas, and Deborah Warren

First edition 2009

Library of Congress Cataloging-in-Publication Data is available.
Library of Congress Catalog Card Number 2008934344
ISBN 978-0-7636-3615-9

2 4 6 8 10 9 7 5 3 1

Printed in China

This book was typeset in Woodland.
The illustrations were done in gouache.

Candlewick Press
99 Dover Street
Somerville, Massachusetts 02144

visit us at www.candlewick.com

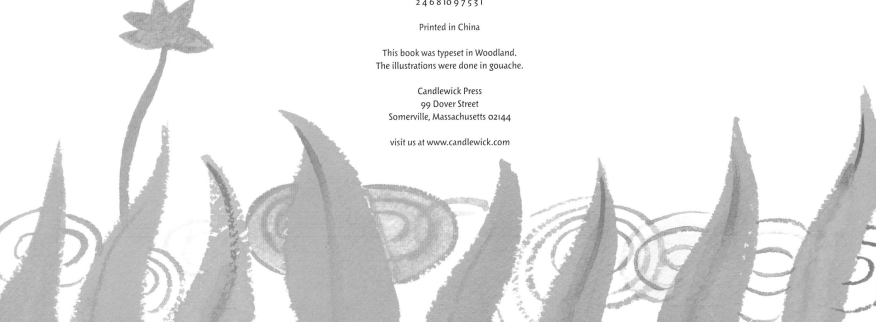

Foo, the Flying Frog

# of Washtub Pond

BELLE YANG

CANDLEWICK PRESS

FROM THE BEGINNING, Foo Frog, Sue-Lin Salamander, and Mao-Mao Mudpuppy were best friends. They began life on the very same day in the very same spot on the banks of Washtub Pond. They also began life the very same size.

But very quickly, Foo grew bigger than his friends.

Now, when they played tug-of-war with a blade of grass,

Foo easily outpulled Sue-Lin.

Though he didn't mean to, when Foo wrestled with Mao-Mao, he often threw him off the lily pad.

At first, Foo's friends didn't mind that Foo was bigger and stronger than they were. They didn't even mind when he threw them farther and deeper into the pond.

But then they noticed that it wasn't just Foo's strength
and size that were growing. His head was growing bigger, too.
He became boastful.

"I must be the biggest animal in the whole wide world,"
he declared one morning.

All that afternoon and into the night, Foo circled Washtub
Pond, pounded on a drum, and chanted, "I am the biggest animal
in the whole wide world! I am the biggest animal in the whole
wide world!"

By morning, Foo was so tired from bragging, he fell deeply asleep in the bulrushes.

"Finally, it's quiet again!" said Sue-Lin. "Now I can get some sleep."

"Yes, and now I can play my flute in peace," chirped Mao-Mao.

Just as the two friends were relaxing, an ear-bursting *Praaah!* shattered the silence.

Sue-Lin and Mao-Mao dived — *putong, putong* — into the water. Carefully, they peered out from underneath their lily pad.

"*Waaah!* What a big animal!" cried Mao-Mao.

"I've never seen anything bigger!" cried Sue-Lin. "No way could Foo out-tug *that* animal."

"No way could Foo throw *that* animal in wrestling!" Mao-Mao chimed in.

The two friends watched the enormous creature slurp up water with its long nose.

Finally it stomped away — *Kuong! Kuong! Kuong!* — its footsteps rattling the lotus pods.

The noise woke up Foo. He hopped out of the bulrushes.

"Foo! Foo!" Sue-Lin cried. "The biggest animal in the world came to visit while you were napping!"

"Yes, its back was as large as a mountain!" cried Mao-Mao.

"Was the animal as big as this?" Foo asked, and he sucked in some air to puff himself up.

"Bigger!" said Sue-Lin. "Its legs were as thick as logs."

"Its snout was longer than the longest lotus root," said Mao-Mao.

Foo sucked in more air.

"It was bigger!" cried Mao-Mao.

"B-bigger?" Foo stammered. He sucked in still more air.

There was now so much hot air in Foo's stretchy belly that
a puff of wind lifted him off the ground as though he were a
balloon. Another gust came along, lifted him up over the
bamboo, and blew him, higher and higher, into the sky.

"Foo, let out some air!" cried Sue-Lin and Mao-Mao. But
Foo could not hear them. He was too high up. All that his
friends could see of him was a tiny green speck.

"Gee," said Sue-Lin, "Foo is really quite small, after all."

The wind carried Foo over fields and farms, rivers and rice paddies. Pigs, donkeys, water buffalo, goats, and horses dotted the meadow below him.

"*Hnh*," Foo snorted. "The animals of the world are no bigger than tadpoles and gnats. I am indeed the biggest creature in the whole wide—"

Just then, a great white heron flew by and snatched up Foo in its beak.

"*Waaah!*" screamed Foo. A little hot air whistled out of him—*shuuuuuu.*

"*Graaak!*" croaked the heron, and he spat Foo out. "You're a nasty-flavored frog!"

Foo fell down, down from the sky and landed with a *budong!* in the ocean.

A huge fish rose to the surface and grabbed Foo in its jaws.

"Waaah!" screamed Foo. More hot air whistled out of him—
shuuuuuu.

"Phooey!" said the fish, and she spat Foo out. "What an awful,
sour-tasting thing!"

No sooner had the fish let go of Foo than a giant sea turtle
gripped him in its beak.

"*Waaah!*" shrieked Foo. "What an enormous monster!"
The last of the hot air was squeezed out of Foo — *shuuuuuu.*
"Blah," said the sea turtle, "what a vile-tasting critter!"
And with a *peiii!* he spat Foo far out onto dry land, right onto
the banks of Washtub Pond.

As Foo lay on the ground, gasping, a colossal foot came down nearly right on top of him.

"*Waaah!*" wailed Foo, staring up at the big, long trunk and giant floppy ears of what must truly have been the biggest animal in the whole world. "Please don't eat me!" he begged.

"*Praaah!*" said the elephant, rubbing its mountainous back against a banana tree. "Why would I eat a tiny, shriveled-up thing like you?"

Then the elephant stomped away into the jungle — *Kuong! Kuong! Kuong!* — making the ground quiver and leaving Foo all alone, shrunken and miserable.

Sue-Lin and Mao-Mao were foraging for snails when they tripped over a lump in the grass.

"Hey, what's this wrinkled green thing?" said Mao-Mao.

"It's Foo!" shouted Sue-Lin. "Foo, you're back!"

"Whatever happened to you?" asked Mao-Mao.

Foo just croaked in exhaustion.

Sue-Lin fed him mosquito larvae. "Foo, you'll grow big again in no time," she said.

Blinking back a tear, Foo replied, "I learned that I am nothing but a very small frog in a very big world."

"Foo, you are the perfect size," said Mao-Mao, "for a frog."

"Yes," said Sue-Lin, "and you are the perfect size for a friend."

And Foo, the Flying Frog of Washtub Pond, swelled bigger and bigger with happiness, till he was his own right size again.